Groundwood Books / House of Anansi Press
groundwoodbooks.com

We gratefully acknowledge for their financial support of our publishing
program the Canada Council for the Arts, the Ontario Arts Council and
the Government of Canada.

Canada Council   Conseil des Arts
for the Arts   du Canada

ONTARIO ARTS COUNCIL
CONSEIL DES ARTS DE L'ONTARIO
an Ontario government agency
un organisme du gouvernement de l'Ontario

With the participation of the Government of Canada
Avec la participation du gouvernement du Canada | Canadä

Library and Archives Canada Cataloguing in Publication
Title: Night walk / Sara O'Leary ; illustrated by Ellie Arscott.
Names: O'Leary, Sara, author. | Arscott, Ellie, illustrator.
Identifiers: Canadiana (print) 20190228113 | Canadiana (ebook)
20190228121 | ISBN 9781554987962 (hardcover) |
ISBN 9781554987979 (EPUB) | ISBN 9781773064253 (Kindle)
Classification: LCC PS8579.L293 N54 2020 | DDC jC813/.54—dc23

The illustrations were done in watercolor and ink pen on paper.
Design by Michael Solomon
Printed and bound in China

FSC
www.fsc.org

MIX
Paper from
responsible sources
FSC® C144853

This book is for Miriam Barry.
I will always be so grateful to your
mother, Sheila. And she was always
so very proud of you.
— S.O'L.

Thank you to my family for their
endless encouragement; to Michael,
Nan and Groundwood for making a
wish come true with this book;
and to my dad, who taught me to stop
and take in the magic of the world.
— E.A.

NIGHT WALK

Written by
Sara O'Leary

Illustrated by
Ellie Arscott

Groundwood Books
House of Anansi Press
Toronto   Berkeley

The time was long past when I should have been
dreaming, but I lay in my bed, owl-eyed and awake.

Dad appeared in my doorway.
 "Can't sleep?" he asked. "Come on. We'll go for a walk."

My little brother was in the crib with his bottom up in the air as usual.

My big sister was in her bunk with the ladder pulled up after her.

And in the living room, my mother was sleeping
in front of the television because she likes to watch
movies with her eyes shut.

I had been out after dark before,
but this time was different.

We were going
out just to be out.
And it was just
Dad and me.

We walked from one island of light to the next like explorers.
Seen by night, everything seemed new and strange.

When the world is dark, the lighted windows of people's houses mean that you see everything you don't see by day.

In one house there were lights on in every room.

The next house only had one lonely
light shining.

I saw for the first time that the sad-looking
woman's shop was also a home.
And that she wasn't always sad.

In one house a big family was eating a meal too late for supper and too early for breakfast. They were so happy it made me happy too.

Was it always like this when I was asleep in
my bed at night? So many people everywhere!

"When I was a child we lived in the country," said Dad. "I could walk for miles without ever seeing another house or a neighbor."

I've always lived here, surrounded by
people I know and people I don't know.

I can't imagine living
anywhere else.

I belong here and here belongs to me.

I am home.